Hans Christian Andersen

Stories and Fairy Tales

The Steadfast Tin Soldier

The Shepherdess and the Chimney Sweep

The Princess on the Pea

The Tinderbox

What Father Does is Always Right

The Swineherd

The Pixie at the Grocer's

The Little Match Girl

The Emperor's New Clothes

The Sweethearts

The Fir Tree

Twelve by Coach

HANS CHRISTIAN ANDERSEN

Stories and Fairy Tales

HANS CHRISTIAN ANDERSEN

Stories and Fairy Tales
selected, translated
and illustrated by
Erik Blegvad

HEINEMANN

THIS IS THE HOUSE WHERE WE BELIEVE H C ANDERSEN WAS BORN

First published in Great Britain 1993
by Heinemann Young Books
an imprint of Reed Consumer Books Limited
Michelin House,81 Fulham Road, London SW3 6RB
and Auckland, Melbourne, Singapore and Toronto
Translation and illustrations copyright © 1993 Erik Blegvad
ISBN 0 434 92904 2
A CIP catalogue record for this book is available at the British Library
Printed and bound in Italy by L.E.G.O. S.p.a., Vicenza

CONTENTS

INTRODUCTION

MY PARENTS READ ME his stories when I was a child. My grandfather actually saw the great man walking in the street in Copenhagen. Not an unusual introduction to the world of Hans Christian Andersen for a Dane of my generation. His stories are an important part of our lives; we always carry them and his name in our hearts.

THIS IS THE HOUSE WHERE H C ANDERSEN GREW UP UNTIL 1819

His mother called him Christian, but to the rest of Denmark he is always H. C. Andersen. Never Hans Christian and never, never Hans Andersen. He was born in 1805 in Odense on the island of Funen to loving parents whose lives were crippled by poverty, ignorance and superstition. He left home when only fourteen, alone and with just a few Skillings in his pocket, to seek his fortune in Copenhagen. Here, after some desperate years, his talents were brought to the attention of the King who, obeying an old Danish custom, granted him a scholarship for an education. In 1828 he passed his examinations and began to make the career which, largely through his own efforts and talents, made him world-famous by the time he died in 1875.

He wrote poems, dramas and novels as well as memoirs in which his wondrous fairytale life is only slightly idealised. Many works were translated into other languages and on his frequent travels abroad he soon found himself a valued guest in the royal and princely households of Europe.

In 1835, he published the first of his one hundred and fifty-six tales for children. Whereas his early novels had made him famous, these tales made him immortal. His visits to the great capitals of Europe became triumphant entries. The Brothers Grimm, the poet Heinrich Heine, Clara and Robert Schumann, Mendelssohn, Alexandre Dumas, Victor Hugo, Dickens and the Brownings were just a few of his many foreign admirers and friends. These fairy tales are not only for children. Many of them are about himself; his struggles and triumphs appear in various guises, but they speak with great clarity of universal truths and human qualities; courage and humour, love and fidelity, as well as evil and suffering. We Danes consider them a national treasure. Of course, we read them in Danish, preferably in editions with the 19th century drawings by Vilhelm Pedersen and Lorenz Frølich. I have tried to put the love and respect I feel for those two artists in my illustrations for this book.

It is a sad fact that something is invariably lost in translation, even between related languages such as Danish and English. It is my great good fortune to be, like H. C. Andersen, a Dane. His is also my mother-tongue and I understand his every word and innuendo. If the English in these translations sounds old-fashioned, well, so does the original Danish. If it reads at all well, it is in large measure due to the invaluable help of my American wife, Lenore, who is a writer, and to the many wise suggestions of my editor, Jane Fior, who is English. Any errors are, of course, mine, the illustrator's. As for the illustrations, enough said. They are all drawn by me, the translator.

ERIK BLEGVAD

London May 1993

THE STEADFAST TIN SOLDIER

THERE WERE ONCE twenty-five tin soldiers. They were all brothers because they were made from an old tin spoon. They shouldered arms and faced straight ahead; red and blue in their splendid uniforms. The first sound they ever heard in this world, as the lid of their box was removed, was "Tin soldiers!" shouted by a little boy clapping his hands. He had been given them for his birthday and now was arranging them on the table. Each soldier looked exactly like the next, except for one who was a bit different. He had only one leg as he was the last to be cast and there had not been enough tin. Yet he stood as steadily on his one as the others on their two, and it is precisely he who is going to be of interest.

On the table where they had been arranged were many other toys. But the most noticeable was a lovely paper castle. Through the tiny windows you could see straight into the rooms. Outside small trees were placed around a little mirror, which was meant to look like a lake. Wax swans swam on it and were mirrored in it. It was all perfectly lovely, but yet loveliest of all was a little lady standing at the open castle door. She was also cut out of paper, but she had on a skirt of the clearest muslin and wore a narrow little blue ribbon over her shoulder. In the middle of that sat a glittering sequin as big as her whole face. The little lady stretched out both her arms, because she was a dancer, and one leg was lifted so high in the air that the tin soldier couldn't see it at all and believed that, like him, she had only one leg.

"There's the wife for me!" he thought. "But she is very grand, she lives in a castle. All I have is a box and we are twenty-five who share it; it is not the place for her! Yet I must try to make her acquaintance." So he lay down full length behind a snuff-box that stood on the table. From there he had a perfect view of the elegant little dancer, who continued to stand on one leg without losing her balance.

When it was evening, all the other tin soldiers were put back in their box and the people of the house went to bed. Now the toys began to play; they played at going visiting, going to war and giving a ball. The tin soldiers rattled inside their box, for they wanted to join in, but they could not open the lid. The nutcracker did somersaults, and the slate pencil danced on the slate. There was so much noise that the canary woke up and began to add his voice, and that he did in verse. The only two who did not move were the tin soldier and the little dancer. She held herself perfectly erect on tiptoe with both arms outstretched. He was equally steadfast on his one leg; his eyes never left her for a moment.

The clock struck twelve, and snap! the lid jumped off the small box but there was no snuff inside. No, just a little black goblin.

It was very cleverly made.

"Tin soldier!" cried the goblin. "Keep your eyes to yourself!"

But the tin soldier pretended not to have heard.

"All right. Just you wait until tomorrow!" the goblin said.

When morning came, and the children got up, the tin soldier was put by the window, and whether it was the goblin or the draught, suddenly the window flew open and the soldier fell out on his head from the third floor. It was a dreadful fall; his leg pointed straight up in the air and he found himself standing on his bearskin hat with his bayonet stuck down between the paving stones.

The maid and one little boy came down at once to search, but although they nearly stepped on him, they could not see him. Had the tin soldier called, "I'm here!" they probably would have found him, but he considered it unseemly to shout loudly when in uniform.

Then it began to rain, one drop fell after the next, until it turned into a heavy shower. When it was over, two ragamuffins came by.

"Look at that!" said one of them. "There's a tin soldier! Let's send him to sea."

So they made a boat from a newspaper, put the tin soldier in it, and sailed him down the gutter. Both boys ran alongside clapping their hands. Goodness me! What waves there were in that gutter, and what a current! Of course it had been quite a shower. The paper boat tossed up and down, and now and then it turned so swiftly that the tin soldier trembled. But he remained steadfast, never changed his expression, looked straight on ahead and shouldered his gun.

Suddenly the boat drifted into a long drain. It was as dark in there as if he were in his box.

"I wonder where I'm going?" he thought. "Yes, yes, it's all the goblin's doing! Oh, if only the little dancer were sitting here in the boat with me, I wouldn't mind if it were twice as dark as it is."

Just then a large water rat who lived in the drain appeared.

"Do you have a passport?" asked the rat. "Show us your passport!"

But the tin soldier said nothing and gripped his gun even tighter. The boat sped along and the rat after it. Ooh! How it gnashed its teeth and shouted to sticks and straws, "Stop him! Stop him! He hasn't paid the toll! He hasn't shown his passport!"

But the current ran faster and faster; the tin soldier could already see daylight ahead where the drain ended. He could also hear a roaring sound, a sound that could easily frighten a brave man. For imagine, where the drain ended, the water poured out into a big canal. To him it was as dangerous as it would be for us to sail over a great waterfall.

He was already so close that he could not stop. The boat shot out, and the poor tin soldier held himself as erect as he could. No one should accuse him of having blinked an eye. The boat swirled around three, four times and filled with water; it was bound to sink.

The tin soldier stood in water up to his neck and the boat sank deeper and deeper; the paper fell apart more and more. Now the water closed over his head – and at that moment when he thought of the lovely little dancer whom he never would see again, the tin soldier seemed to hear:

> *"On, on, warrior!*
> *On to meet thy death!"*

Now the paper fell completely to pieces and the tin soldier tumbled through it. At once he was swallowed by a large fish. My, it was dark in there! It was even worse than in the drain and it was so very narrow. But the tin soldier was steadfast and lay full length, shouldering his gun.

The fish darted about making the most dreadful contortions. At last it lay quite still, and a flash passed through it like lightning. Bright daylight shone and somebody shouted loudly, "The tin soldier!" The fish had been caught, taken to market, sold and brought to the kitchen where the cook had cut it open with a big knife. She gripped the soldier by the waist in two fingers and carried him into the sitting room where everybody wanted to see the remarkable man who had travelled about in the stomach of a fish. But the tin soldier did not let it go to his head. They put him on the table and there – Now, what strange things happen in this world! The tin soldier was in the very same room where he had been before. He saw the very same children and the toys on the table, the pretty castle with the lovely little dancer who still stood on one leg and held the other one high in the air; she too was steadfast. This moved the tin soldier. He could have wept tin, but that would not have been proper. He gazed at her and she gazed at him, but they said nothing.

Suddenly one of the small boys took the soldier and threw him straight on the fire. He gave no reason for it at all, it was surely the goblin in the box who was to blame.

The tin soldier stood there, glowing brightly, and felt a dreadful heat, though whether it was caused by the fire or by love, he did not know. He had lost all his bright colours, though whether this had happened on his journey or from grief, no one could say. He looked at the little lady, she looked at him, and he felt himself melting, but he still bore himself erect, shouldering his gun. Then a door opened, the draught lifted up the dancer and she blew like a sylph straight into the fire to the tin soldier, she flared up in a blaze and was gone. Then the tin soldier melted down to a lump and next morning when the maid emptied the grate, she found him in the shape of a little tin heart. As for the dancer, only the sequin was left, and that had been burnt as black as coal.

THE SHEPHERDESS AND THE CHIMNEYSWEEP

HAVE YOU EVER SEEN a really old wooden cupboard, quite black with age and carved with scrolls and foliage? Just such a cupboard once stood in a sitting room. It had been inherited from Great-grandmother. It was carved with roses and tulips from top to bottom, and was full of the most peculiar scrolls, from amongst which stags' heads with many antlers peered out. But in the middle of the cupboard was carved an entire man. True he looked somewhat laughable, and he was indeed laughing, although you couldn't call it a real laugh. He had goat's legs, little horns in his forehead and a long beard. The children of the house called him General-Commander-Sergeant Billy Goat's Legs, because it's a difficult name to say, and there are not many who attain that rank. It must also have been quite a feat to have carved him out. However, there he was!

He always looked across at the table under the mirror, for there stood a lovely little porcelain shepherdess. She had gilt shoes, a frock prettily tucked up with a red rose, a golden hat and a shepherd's crook. She was adorable! Close to her stood a little

20

chimneysweep, as black as coal, also made of porcelain. He was just as clean and neat as anyone else. It was pure chance that he was a chimneysweep. The man who made him could just as easily have made him a prince.

He stood there so neatly with his ladder, and with a face as pink as a girl's, though really that was a mistake, he should have been a little bit sooty. He stood very close to the shepherdess. They had both been put where they stood, and as they had been placed there, they had become engaged. They suited each other. Both were young, they were made of the same porcelain, and both were equally fragile.

Close to them was yet another figure, three times their size. He was an old Chinese man and he could nod. He was also made of porcelain and he said he was the grandfather of the little shepherdess, though this was difficult to prove. He also claimed to be her guardian and so when General-Commander-Sergeant Billy Goat's Legs proposed to the little shepherdess he nodded.

"He will make you a fine husband," said the old Chinese man.

"He's a man who I'm almost certain is made of mahogany. He'll make you Mrs General-Commander-Sergeantess Billy Goat's Legs. His whole cupboard is filled with silver, quite apart from what he has stowed away in secret hiding places!"

"I don't want to be in that dark cupboard!" said the little shepherdess, "I've heard it said that he has eleven porcelain wives in there already."

"Then you can be the twelfth!" said the Chinese man. "Tonight, as soon as the old cupboard begins to creak, we shall have the wedding, upon my honour as a Chinese." And he nodded his head and fell asleep. But the little shepherdess wept and looked at her heart's beloved, the porcelain chimneysweep.

"I think I must ask you," she said, "to come with me out into the wide world, for we cannot stay here!"

"I want only what you want!" said the little chimneysweep. "Let's leave at once. I am sure I can support you by my profession!"

"I wish we were safely down off the table!" she said, "I shall not be happy until we're out in the wide world!"

He consoled her and showed her where to put her tiny foot on the carved edges and the gilded foliage down around the table leg. He used his ladder too and finally they found themselves standing on the floor, but when they looked over to the old cupboard there was such a to-do. All the carved stags were poking their heads out even further, raising their antlers and craning their necks. The General-Commander-Sergeant Billy Goat's Legs sprang high in the air shouting over to the old Chinese man. "Look, they are running away, look!"

The shepherdess and the chimneysweep were frightened by this and jumped into an open drawer under the window seat.

Here they found three or four incomplete packs of cards and a small toy theatre which had been set up after a fashion. A play was being performed and all the Queens of Diamonds, Hearts, Clubs and Spades sat in the front row fanning themselves. Behind them stood all the Knaves showing off their two heads, both above and below, as they have them on playing cards. The plot dealt with a couple who were not allowed to marry and it made the shepherdess weep, it was so like her own story.

"I cannot bear this!" she said. "I must get out of the drawer!" But when they stood on the floor again and looked up at the table the old Chinese man was awake. His whole body was rocking for, you see, his lower part was made all in one piece.

"The old Chinese man is coming!" cried the little shepherdess, and she fell to her porcelain knees in sorrow.

"I have an idea!" said the chimneysweep. "Let's climb into the large pot-pourri jar in the corner. There we can lie on roses and lavender and throw salt in his eyes if he comes."

"That wouldn't do any good," she said. "Besides, I happen to know that the old Chinese man and the pot-pourri jar used to be engaged and some affection always remains after such a relationship! No, we have no choice, but to go out into the wide world."

"Are you really so brave, that you'll leave with me for the wide world?" asked the chimneysweep. "Have you considered how huge it is, and that we may never return here?"

"I have," she said.

The chimneysweep then looked hard at her and he said, "My way goes through the chimney. Are you really brave enough to crawl with me through the stove, both through the flue and the pipe? If we do, we will be in the chimney and that's where I am in my element. We will climb up and up, so high that they will never catch us, all the way up to the top where there's a hole leading out to the wide world."

And he led her over to the stove door.

"It looks black," she said, but she followed him all the same, both through the flue and the pipe, where it was pitch black as night.

"Now we are in the chimney!" said he, "and look! look! there's a lovely star shining above!"

And so there was! A real star in the sky, shining straight down on them as if it wished to show them the way. They crawled and they crept. It was a dreadful climb, higher and higher, but he lifted and helped, holding her and showing her the places where it was best to put her tiny porcelain feet. Finally they reached the very rim of the chimneypot and here they sat down. They were dreadfully tired and no wonder.

The sky with all its stars was above them and all the roofs of the city below. They could see far around as they looked out into the wide world. The poor shepherdess had never imagined it like that;

she leaned her little head against her chimneysweep and then she wept so that the gilt peeled off her waistband.

"It's too much!" she said. "I can't bear it! The world is too big! I wish I were back on the little table under the mirror. I shall never be happy until I'm back there again. I have followed you out into the wide world. Now you can please follow me home again if you care for me at all!"

The chimneysweep talked sensibly to her, talked about the old Chinese man and about General-Commander-Sergeant Billy Goat's Legs, but she sobbed so heartrendingly and so kissed her little chimneysweep, that all he could do was give in even though it was wrong to do so.

And so, with great difficulty, they climbed back down inside the chimney, and they crawled through the pipe and the flue, and it wasn't at all pleasant, until they stood inside the dark stove. They lurked behind the door to find out what was going on in the sitting room. All was still. They looked out: alas, in the middle of the floor lay the old Chinese man. He had fallen off the table trying to chase after them, and he was lying broken in three pieces. His whole back had come off in one piece and his head had rolled into a corner. General-Commander-Sergeant Billy Goat's Legs stood where he had always stood, thinking it over.

"How horrible!" said the little shepherdess, "Old Grandfather has been smashed to pieces and it's all our fault! I shall never get over it!" and she wrung her tiny little hands.

"He can be mended!" said the chimneysweep. "He can easily be glued! Don't get so excited! If they cement him in the back and give him a nice rivet in the neck, he will be just as good as new and quite as unpleasant as he was before."

"Do you think so?" she asked. Then they climbed back up on to the table where they used to stand.

"Look how far this got us," said the chimneysweep. "We could have spared ourselves the trouble."

"If only we could have old Grandfather fixed!" said the shepherdess. "Would it really be so very expensive?"

He *was* repaired. The family had him cemented in the back and given a nice rivet in his neck. He was as good as new, only he could no longer nod his head.

"You seem to have become quite haughty since you were broken to bits!" General-Commander-Sergeant Billy Goat's Legs said to him, "though I can't see that it's much to be stuck up about! Am I to have her or am I not?"

The chimneysweep and the little shepherdess looked anxiously at the old Chinese man. They were so afraid that he might nod, but he couldn't and he did not like to admit to a stranger that he would have a rivet in his neck forever.

And so they were pronounced porcelain man and wife. They blessed Grandfather's rivet and worshipped each other until the day they broke.

THE PRINCESS ON THE PEA

Once upon a time there was a prince; he wanted a princess but it had to be a *real* princess. So he travelled all over the world to find one, but everywhere he went something was wrong. There were princesses enough, but were they real princesses? That was the problem. There was always something not quite right. So he came home again, feeling very sad; he would so much have liked to find a real princess.

One night there was a terrible storm. There was thunder and lightning, and the rain came pouring down – it was quite dreadful! Someone was heard knocking on the city gate and the old king went to open it.

Outside stood a princess, but goodness, what a sight she was from the rain and the cruel weather. Water was running from her hair and down her clothes. It ran in at the toes of her shoes and out at the heels, and still she said she was a real princess.

"Well, we shall soon see about that!" thought the old queen. She didn't say anything but went to the bedroom, took all the bedclothes off and put a pea on the bottom of the bed. Then she took twenty mattresses and put them on top of the pea and a further twenty eiderdown quilts on top of the mattresses. This was where the princess was to lie that night.

In the morning they asked her how she had slept.

"Oh – so dreadfully badly!" said the princess, "I hardly shut an eye the whole night long. Goodness knows what was in that bed! I was lying on something so hard that I'm black and blue all over! It was perfectly dreadful!"

Now they could see that she was a real princess for she had felt the pea through twenty mattresses and twenty eiderdown quilts. Only a real princess could have such tender skin.

The prince took her as his wife, because he knew that he had a real princess, and the pea was put in a museum where it is still to be seen, if nobody has taken it.

Now, what did you think of that for a story!

THE TINDERBOX

A SOLDIER CAME MARCHING along a country road, one, two! one, two! He had his knapsack on his back and a sword at his side, for he had been to the wars, and now he was going home. But then he met an old witch on the road. She was very ugly – her lower lip hung right down on her chest.

She said, "Good evening, soldier! What a fine sword you have and what a big knapsack! You are a proper soldier to be sure! Now you shall have as much money as you want!"

"I thank you, old witch!" said the soldier.

"Do you see that big tree?" said the witch, pointing to one growing next to where they stood. "Inside, it is quite hollow. You must climb up to the top and there you will find a hole in the trunk; slide through it and you will come deep down inside the tree. I will tie a rope around your waist so I can pull you back up again when you shout for me."

"What am I to do down in the tree?" asked the soldier.

"Fetch money!" said the witch. "Now listen. Once you reach the bottom of the tree, you will be in a large hall. It's quite light there, for over a hundred lamps are burning. You will see three doors.

30

You can open them; the key is in the lock. If you go into the first room, you'll see a large chest in the middle of the floor. On top of it will sit a dog. He has eyes as big as teacups, but never you mind! I'll give you my blue-checked apron; you can spread it on the floor. Go straight up and take the dog, sit him on my apron, open the chest and take out as many pennies as you want. They are all copper. However, if you prefer silver, go into the next room. In there sits a dog with eyes as big as millwheels, but never you mind! Sit him on my apron and help yourself to the money! On the other hand, if it's gold you want, you can have that too, as much as you can carry if you go into the next room. There the dog sitting on the chest has eyes as big as the Round Tower. That's a real dog, I can tell you! But never mind that! Just sit him on my apron, so he won't harm you, and help yourself to as much gold as you want from the chest!"

"That doesn't sound so bad," said the soldier. "But what about you, old witch? I imagine you'll want something too."

"No," said the witch. "I don't want a single penny. Just bring me the old tinderbox which my grandmother forgot when she was last down there."

"Well, then! Let me have that rope around me!" said the soldier.

"Here you are," said the witch, "and here's my blue-checked apron."

The soldier climbed up the tree, slipped into the hole, and now found himself, as the witch had said, down in the big hall, where the many hundred lamps were burning.

He opened the first door. Ooh! There sat the dog with eyes as big as teacups, staring at him.

"You're a fine fellow!" said the soldier. He sat the dog on the witch's apron and took as many copper pennies as he could fit in his pockets, closed the chest, put the dog back on top and walked into the next room.

Well, there sat the dog with eyes as big as millwheels!

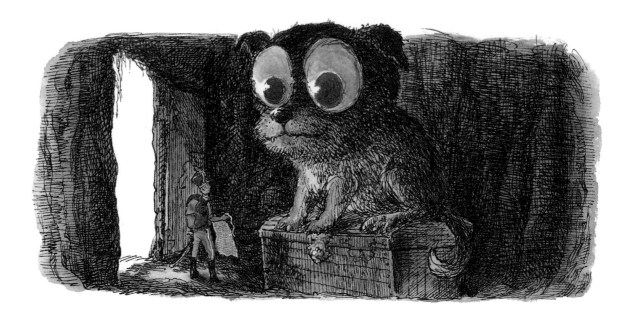

"You shouldn't stare at me like that!" said the soldier, "you'll hurt your eyes!" He sat the dog on the witch's apron, but when he saw the piles of silver coins in the chest, he threw out the copper and filled his pockets and knapsack with pure silver.

Now he went into the third room! Goodness gracious! How horrible! The dog in there really did have two eyes as big as the Round Tower! And they spun round in his head like two carriage wheels!

"Good evening!" said the soldier and touched his cap, for he had never seen such a dog before; but after looking at him for a bit he thought, that's enough of that. He lifted him down on the floor and opened up the chest. Mercy me! What a lot of gold there was! With it he could buy up the entire city of Copenhagen, all the pastry cook's sugar pigs, and all the tin soldiers, whips and rocking-horses in the world! Yes, that certainly was a hoard! Now the soldier threw out all the silver he had stuffed into his pockets and his knapsack, and took gold instead – yes, all his pockets, his pack, his cap and his boots were filled so that he could barely walk! Now he had money! He put the dog back on top of the chest, shut the door and called up through the tree, "You can pull me out now, old witch!"

"Have you got the tinderbox with you?" asked the witch.

"I must admit," said the soldier, "that I completely forgot," and he went to get it. The witch hauled him up and again he stood in the road, with pockets, boots, knapsack and cap all filled with money.

"What are you going to do with that tinderbox?" asked the soldier.

"Mind your own business," said the witch. "You have your money now! Just give me the tinderbox!"

"Fiddlesticks!" said the soldier. "Tell me at once what you want it for, or I'll draw my sword and cut your head off!"

"No!" said the witch.

So the soldier cut her head off and there she lay! He tied the money up in her apron, slung it on his back in a bundle, put the tinderbox in his pocket and walked straight into town.

It was a splendid town and he moved into the most splendid inn, ordered the very best room and all his favourite food, for he was rich now that he had all that money.

The servant who was to shine his boots, naturally thought they were funny old boots for such a wealthy gentleman, for the soldier had not yet had time to buy new ones. The next day he bought himself a pair of boots and a set of decent clothes. Now that the soldier had become a fine gentleman, people told him about all the festivities going on in their town, and about their king and what a pretty princess his daughter was.

"Where can she be seen?" asked the soldier.

"She can't be seen at all!" everyone said. "She lives in a large copper castle surrounded by many walls and towers! No one except the king dares to go in or out of it because a fortune teller has said that she will marry a common soldier and this does not please him."

I'd like to have a look at her, thought the soldier, but of course that would not be allowed.

He led a merry life. He went to the theatre, drove in the king's gardens and gave much money to the poor. That was a handsome thing to do but he knew from the old days how painful it is not to have a penny to your name. Now that he was rich, he had fine clothes, and made lots of friends who all said what a nice fellow he was – a real cavalier – and the soldier enjoyed that! But as he spent money every day and never had any coming in, he was finally left with only two pennies and had to move out of the lovely room where he used to live and move upstairs to a tiny little room under the roof. He had to shine his own boots and mend them with a darning needle, and none of his friends came to see him any more because there were so many stairs to climb.

It was a very dark evening and he couldn't even afford to buy a candle, but he suddenly remembered that there was a small stump in the tinderbox he had taken from the hollow tree when the witch had helped him out. He fetched the tinderbox and the candle stump, but just as he struck a light and sparks flew from the flint, his door burst open and the dog from inside the tree with eyes as big as teacups stood before him and said, "What does my master command?"

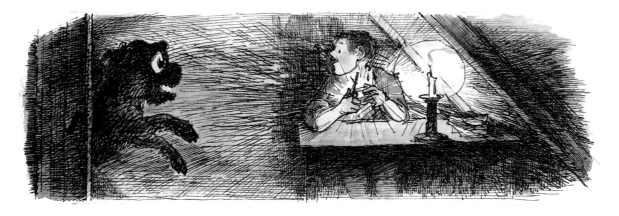

"What's this?" said the soldier. "That's quite a tinderbox, if it answers my every wish! Get me some money!" he said to the dog, and hey presto it was gone! And hey presto it came back carrying a large bag full of coppers in its mouth.

Now the soldier found out what a splendid tinderbox it was! If he struck once, the dog sitting on the chest with the copper money appeared. If he struck twice, the one that sat on the silver money appeared, and if he struck three times, the one with the gold appeared. The soldier was able to move back downstairs to the beautiful room, put on fine clothes, and at once be taken up by all his old friends who again made a great fuss over him.

One night, he thought how very odd it is that nobody is allowed to see that princess! She's supposed to be so lovely. Everybody says so. But what good is it if all she does is sit inside that great copper castle with its many towers. Can I really not see her? Now, where did I put my tinderbox! And he struck a light and hey presto out came the dog with eyes as big as teacups.

"I know it's the middle of the night," said the soldier, "but I would so much like to see the princess, just for a moment."

The dog was already out of the door, and in the twinkling of an eye, it returned with the princess. She sat asleep on the dog's back and was so lovely that anyone could see that she was a real princess.

The soldier could not help himself, he had to kiss her. For he was a real soldier.

The dog then ran back with the princess, but in the morning, at breakfast, when the king and the queen were pouring tea, the princess said that she had dreamt such a strange dream during the night about a dog and a soldier. She had ridden on the dog and the soldier had kissed her.

"That's a fine story, I must say," said the queen. And she told one of the old ladies-in-waiting to keep watch by the princess's bed that night, to see if it really was a dream or not.

The soldier longed to see the lovely princess once again, and so the dog came that night, took her and ran away as fast as it could. But the old lady-in-waiting put on her gumboots and ran just as fast behind them. When she saw them disappear inside a large house she thought, now I know where it is, and with a piece of chalk she made a great big cross on the door. She then went home to bed, and the dog returned with the princess. When it saw that a cross had been chalked on the soldier's door, it also took a piece of chalk and put crosses on all the doors of the town. This was a clever thing to do for now the lady-in-waiting would not be able to find the right door, as there were crosses on them all.

Early the next morning, the king and the queen, the old lady-in-waiting and all the officers came to find out where the princess had been.

"Here it is!" said the king, when he saw the first door with a cross.

"No, my sweet husband!" said the queen looking at the next door.

"But there's one and there's another one!" said everybody, as they saw there were crosses on every door. They realized then it was no use searching.

However, the queen was a very wise woman who knew more than how to ride in a coach. She took her big golden scissors, cut up a piece of silk and made it into a pretty little purse. She filled it with tiny buckwheat seeds, tied it to the princess's back, and when that was done, she cut a little hole in the bottom so that the seeds would sprinkle on the road the princess took.

At night the dog came again, took the princess on its back and ran with her to the soldier who was so fond of her and so wished he were a prince so that he could have her for his wife.

The dog did not notice how the seed sprinkled all the way from the castle to the soldier's window, where it leapt up the wall with the princess. In the morning, the king and the queen had no trouble finding out where their daughter had been, so they had the soldier arrested and put in prison.

There he sat. Oh, how dark, how dull it was! And they kept saying to him, "Tomorrow you'll be hanged." This was not a nice thing to hear; and he didn't have his tinderbox with him, for he had left it back at the inn.

In the morning, looking through the iron bars of the small window, he saw people hurrying out of town to see him hanged. He heard drums and saw soldiers marching. Everybody was running including a cobbler's boy in a leather apron and slippers. He rushed by at such a gallop that one slipper flew off and fell right up against the wall where the soldier sat looking through the iron bars.

"Hey, you cobbler's boy! Don't be in such a hurry," the soldier called to him. "Nothing will happen before I arrive! But would you mind running back to where I used to live and fetch me my tinderbox. I'll give you fourpence. But you'll have to get a move on!"

The boy wanted the fourpence very much indeed and so darted off to fetch the tinderbox, and gave it to the soldier. Yes now we'll hear what happened!

Outside the town, a large gallows had been built. Around it stood the soldiers and hundreds and thousands of people. The king and queen sat on a fine throne opposite the judge and the whole town council.

The soldier was already standing on the ladder, but when they were about to put the noose round his neck, he said that surely it was customary to allow a sinner one last wish before he was executed. He would so much like to smoke a pipe of tobacco – after all, it would be the last pipe he smoked in this world.

Well, the king did not want to say no to that, and so the soldier took his tinderbox and struck a light once, twice, three times! And there stood all the dogs, the one with eyes as big as teacups, the one with eyes like millwheels and the one with eyes as big as the Round Tower.

"Help me now, so I won't be hanged!" commanded the soldier, and so the dogs flew at the judges and the whole town council, and taking some by the legs and some by the nose they tossed them so high in the air that when they fell down, they were dashed to pieces.

"I won't, I won't be tossed," said the king, but the largest dog took both him and the queen and tossed them after all the others. Then the soldier became frightened and all the people shouted, "Little soldier, you shall be our king and have the lovely princess to be your wife!"

They put the soldier in the king's coach, and the three dogs danced in front shouting "Hurrah!" The boys whistled and the soldiers presented arms. The princess came out of the copper castle and was made queen and she liked that! The wedding lasted for eight whole days, and the dogs sat at the table with the guests and rolled their eyes.

WHAT FATHER DOES IS ALWAYS RIGHT

Now I SHALL TELL YOU A STORY that I heard when I was little. Since then, every time I think of it, it seems to me to have become even nicer; for stories are like many people, they become nicer and nicer with age, and that is so delightful!

Have you ever been to the country? Then perhaps you have seen a really old farmhouse with a thatched roof all covered in moss and herbs. There is a stork's nest on the ridge – for we cannot do without the stork. The walls are crooked, the windows low, in fact only one can be opened. The baking oven sticks out like a fat little stomach and the elder bush leans over the fence where there is a little pond with a duck or some ducklings, right under the gnarled willow tree. And then there is a dog on a chain who barks at anybody and everybody.

There was just such a farmhouse out in the country, and in it lived a couple; a farmer and his wife. Even though their plot was small they nevertheless had set aside a piece of land for their horse which was grazing by the ditch along the road. Father rode it to town and

40

the neighbours borrowed it, repaying him by sometimes lending a hand.

But the couple thought perhaps they would be better off if they sold the horse or traded it for something more useful. But what should it be?

"You understand such things best, Father!" said the wife. "It's market day. Why not ride to town, sell the horse, or exchange it for something better! What you do is always right. Go to market!"

So she knotted his neckerchief, for that was one thing she could do better than he. She tied it with a double bow and it looked quite dashing. Then she brushed his hat with the flat of her hand, kissed him on his warm mouth, and off he rode on the horse which was to be sold or exchanged. Yes, Father understood these things!

The sun was hot, there was not a cloud in the sky. The road billowed with dust; there were so many people on their way to market, in carts, on horseback and on foot. The sun was hot and there was not the slightest bit of shade on the road.

A man was driving a cow along. It was as lovely as a cow can be. "That must give delicious milk!" thought the farmer. The cow would not be a bad exchange if he could get it.

"Hey! You know what, you there with the cow!" he said. "Maybe we two should have a little talk! A horse, I believe, costs more than a cow, but that wouldn't matter! To me a cow would be of more use. Shall we swap?"

"Yes, all right!" said the man with the cow, and the deal was done.

41

So that was that, and although the farmer might now return home – he had, after all, accomplished all he had set out to do – since he had decided to go to market, to market he would go, if only just to see it. And so he walked on with his cow.

He walked fast and the cow walked fast and soon they were walking alongside a man leading a sheep. It was a fine sheep, well fed and well covered with wool.

"I wouldn't mind having that sheep!" thought the farmer. "It wouldn't lack grazing by our ditch, and when winter comes we could have it living indoors. It would really be more sensible for us to graze a sheep rather than a cow." So he said, "Would you care to swap?"

Yes, the man with the sheep was willing, and the deal was done, leaving the farmer to drive his sheep on down the road. There, by a stile, he saw a man with a big goose under his arm.

"That is a fine fellow you have there!" said the farmer. "It has both feathers and fat! It would look just right tethered by our pond! It's exactly what Mother needs for all her potato peelings. She has often said, 'If only we had a goose!' Now she can have one and she *shall* have one! Do you want to swap? I will give you the sheep for the goose and thank you into the bargain!"

Yes, the man agreed, and they made the exchange; the farmer got the goose. As he came closer to the town, the crush on the road increased. It was packed with people and cattle; they trampled all over the road, over the ditch, even on to the toll-keeper's potato patch where his hen was tethered so that if it took fright it wouldn't get lost. It was a handsome short-tailed hen which winked with one eye.

"Cluck-cluck!" it said. What it meant by that, I cannot say, but when the farmer saw it he thought: that is the most beautiful hen I have ever seen. It is even nicer than the vicar's hen. I should like to own it! A hen will always find a grain or two, it can almost fend for itself: I think it would be a good deal if I could exchange it for the goose.

"Shall we swap?" he asked.

"Swap!" said the other, "Yes, why not!" And so they did. The toll-keeper got the goose, the farmer got the hen.

43

By now, he had accomplished quite a lot on that journey to town; and it was hot and he was tired. A drink and a bite to eat was what he needed. He went into an inn and as he entered it, he met a serving boy coming out swinging a full sack on his shoulder.

"What have you got there?" asked the farmer.

"Rotten apples!" answered the boy. "A whole sackful for the pigs."

"That's a lot of apples! I wish Mother could see them. Last year we had but a single apple on the old tree by the peat shed! We wanted to keep it and it stood on the chest until it burst. 'It shows we're people of substance,' Mother used to say. Here she would see something really substantial."

"Well, what do you offer?" asked the boy.

"Offer? I can offer you my hen," and he gave him the hen, got the apples and strode into the tap room, right up to the counter. He leaned his sack of apples against the stove not noticing that it was lit. The room was full of travellers, horse and cattle dealers and two Englishmen, and of course they are so rich that their pockets are bursting with gold. They also like to make bets.

Now listen to this!

Shyss! Shyss! What was that sound coming from the stove? It was the apples beginning to roast.

"What's that?" they asked. Soon they were told the whole story about the horse that was traded for the cow, all the details right down to the rotten apples.

"Well, your wife will wallop you when you get home!" said the Englishmen, "She'll raise the roof!"

"There will be kisses, not wallops!" said the farmer. "She'll say, what Father does is always right!"

"Do you want to bet?" they said. "Gold coins by the barrel?"

"A barrel is too big," said the farmer. "But I could fill a bushel with the apples, myself and Mother. Now *that* would be a generous measure."

"Done!" they said, and the bet was made.

The innkeeper fetched his cart, the Englishmen got in, the farmer got in and the rotten apples were put in too; and off they went to the farmer's house.

"Good evening, Mother!"

"Good evening, Father!"

"I have been trading!"

"Ah, you understand those things!" said the wife and put her arms around him, forgetting the sack and the strangers.

"I traded the horse for a cow!"

"God be praised for the milk!" said the wife, "Now we can have bread and milk, butter and cheese on the table. That was a wonderful deal!"

"Yes, but then I traded the cow for a sheep!"

"That is certainly much better!" said the wife. "You are always so thoughtful. We have grazing enough, now we can have sheep's milk and cheese and woollen stockings, even woollen nightshirts! The cow does not provide that, she sheds her coat. You are a thoughtful husband!"

"But then I traded the sheep for a goose!"

"Are we really to have goose for St Martin's Eve this year, little Father! You always think of my happiness. What a lovely idea! The goose can be tethered and fattened up for St Martin's Eve!"

"But I traded the goose for a hen!" said the husband.

"A hen! That was an excellent exchange," said the wife. "The hen lays eggs, they'll hatch, and we'll have chicks, and a chicken run. That's just what I've always wanted."

"Yes, but I traded the hen for a sack of rotten apples!"

"Now I must kiss you!" said the wife, "Thank you, my own dear husband! Let me tell you something. When you left, I planned to cook you a really special supper; omelette with chives. I had the eggs, but I didn't have any chives. So I went over to the school master's house; I know they have chives there, but his wife is so stingy, (the dear rude soul!) I asked to borrow some. 'Borrow?' said she, 'Nothing grows in our garden, not even a rotten apple! So I can't even lend you that!' Now I can lend her ten, yes, a whole sackful. What a joke, Father!" And she kissed him right on the mouth.

"We like that!" said the Englishmen. "Always downhill and never downhearted. It's well worth the money!" And they filled the bushel with gold coins for the farmer who had not been walloped but kissed.

Yes, it always pays for the wife to see that Father knows best and that whatever he does is right.

So, that was the story! I heard it when I was little, and now you've heard it too, and know that whatever Father does is always right.

THE SWINEHERD

ONCE UPON a time there was a Prince who had no money. He had a kingdom that was small, but big enough to marry on – and marry he would.

All the same it was rather daring of him to ask the Emperor's daughter, "Will you have me?" But dare he did, for he was known far and wide, and there were hundreds of princesses who would have thanked him in the bargain. But do you suppose *she* did? Now we shall hear.

Growing on the grave of the Prince's father was a rose tree – oh, such a lovely rose tree! It bloomed only once every fifth year, and then with just a single blossom that was a rose which smelled so sweet that he who smelled it forgot all care and sorrow.

The Prince also had a nightingale that could sing as if all lovely melodies lived in its little throat. The rose and the nightingale were to be given to the Princess, so both were put in large silver boxes and sent to her.

The Emperor had them carried before him into the grand hall where the Princess was playing "visitors" with her ladies-in-waiting.

48

That was all they ever did. When she saw the silver boxes with the gifts inside, she clapped her hands with joy.

"Oh, I do hope it's a little pussy-cat!" she said – but out came the lovely rose.

"My, how exquisitely it is made!" cried all the ladies.

"It's more than exquisite," said the Emperor. "It's nice!"

But then the Princess touched it, and she almost burst into tears.

"Shame, Papa!" she said. "It's not artificial, it's real!"

"Shame!" cried all the court. "It's real!"

"Let's see what's in the other chest before we get upset," suggested the Emperor, and then the nightingale was brought out. It sang so beautifully that no one could say anything against it.

"*Superbe! Charmant!*" cried the ladies-in-waiting, for they spoke French amongst themselves, one worse than the other.

"How that bird reminds me of our dear departed Empress's music box!" said an elderly courtier. "Ah yes! Exactly the same tone, the same phrasing!"

"Yes indeed," said the Emperor, and he wept like a little child.

"But I can hardly believe that it's real," said the Princess.

"Yes, it is a real bird," said those who had brought it.

"Then let the bird fly away " said the Princess, and on no account would she allow the Prince to call.

But he was not to be put off; he smeared his face with brown and black, pulled his cap down firmly on his head, and knocked on the door.

"Hullo, Emperor!" he said. "Can I get a job here at the castle?"

"Well, we have so many asking –" said the Emperor. "But let's see – I do need someone to look after the swine. We have such a lot of them."

And so the Prince was appointed Imperial Swineherd. He was given a miserable little room by the pigsty, and there he had to stay.

The whole rest of the day he sat and worked. And when evening came, he had a beautiful little iron pot with bells all around it, and as soon as the pot boiled the bells jingled delightfully and played the old tune:

"Ach, du lieber Augustin,
All is gone, gone, gone!"

Yet the cleverest thing about it was that when you held a finger in the steam from the pot, you could instantly smell every meal that was being cooked under every chimney all over town. Now that was something quite different from a rose!

By and by the Princess walked past with her ladies-in-waiting, and when she heard the tune, she stopped delighted, for she too could play *"Ach, du lieber Augustin."* That was the only one she knew, but she played it with one finger.

"That's the one *I* know!" she cried. "This must be an educated swineherd. Listen, go in and ask him how much that instrument costs."

So one of the ladies-in-waiting had to run inside, but she put on wooden shoes.

"How much do you want for that pot?" she asked.

"I want ten kisses from the Princess," answered the swineherd.

"Saints preserve us!" cried the lady-in-waiting.

"It can't be had for less," said the swineherd.

"Well, what does he say?" asked the Princess.

"I really can't repeat it," said the lady-in-waiting. "It's too too dreadful."

"Then you can whisper!"

And whisper she did.

"But he's naughty!" said the Princess and walked away immediately. However, she had only walked a little way when again the bells tinkled charmingly:

> *"Ach, du lieber Augustin,*
> *All is gone, gone, gone!"*

"Look here," said the Princess, "ask him if he will take ten kisses from my ladies-in-waiting."

"No, thank you," said the swineherd. "Ten kisses from the Princess, or I keep my pot."

"Oh, isn't this annoying!" said the Princess. "But you will all have to stand around me, so that no one shall see."

The ladies gathered around her, spreading out their skirts, and the swineherd got his ten kisses and she got the pot.

Well, you never saw such fun! All evening and all day the pot was kept boiling. There wasn't one chimney in the whole city, be it at the Chamberlain's or at the cobbler's, where they didn't know what was being cooked. The ladies-in-waiting danced and clapped their hands.

"We know who is going to have soup and pancakes! We know who is going to have porridge and chops! Isn't it interesting!"

'Very interesting," said the High Stewardess.

"Yes, but not a word about it, for I'm the Emperor's daughter!" replied the Princess.

"Saints preserve us," they all said.

The swineherd – that is to say the Prince, but of course they didn't know any better – let no day go by in idleness. And so he fashioned a rattle. When he swung it around, it played all the waltzes, jigs and polkas known from the beginning of time.

"But it's superb," said the Princess as she walked by. "I have never heard lovelier compositions. Look, go in and ask him how much that instrument costs. But there will be no kissing!"

"He wants a hundred kisses from the Princess," said the lady who had been in to ask.

"I do believe the fellow is mad," said the Princess, and she left. But she had only walked a little way when she stopped again.

"One must encourage the arts," she said. "I am the Emperor's daughter. Tell him he may have ten kisses as yesterday. The rest he can take from my ladies-in-waiting."

"But we would so much rather not," said the ladies.

"That's nonsense!" said the Princess. "If I can kiss him, you can too. Remember I give you your board and keep!" And the lady had to go back in.

"A hundred kisses from the Princess," the swineherd said, "or each keeps his own."

"Stand in front!" the Princess cried. And all the ladies-in-waiting placed themselves in front, and he started kissing.

"Now what is that crowd down at the pigsty?" said the Emperor, who had stepped out on the balcony. He rubbed his eyes and put on his spectacles. "Why, it's the ladies-in-waiting up to their tricks! I'd better get down there!" And he pulled up his slippers at the back, for they were really shoes he had trodden down at the heels.

My, how he hurried!

When he reached the courtyard, he walked very quietly, and the ladies-in-waiting had so much to do counting kisses to see that all was fair – the swineherd should have neither too many nor too few – that they didn't notice the Emperor. He stretched up on his toes.

"What's this!" he cried, when he saw them kissing. And he beat them over their heads with his slipper, at the exact moment when the swineherd received his eighty-sixth kiss.

"Get out!" said the Emperor, for he was angry, and both the Princess and the swineherd were turned out of his empire.

There she stood weeping. The swineherd scolded and the rain came pouring down.

"Alas, poor me!" cried the Princess. "If only I had taken the lovely Prince. Oh, how unhappy I am!"

The swineherd went behind a tree, wiped the black and brown from his face, took off the ugly clothes, and stepped forth in his princely robes, so splendid that the Princess had to curtsy.

"You know," he said, "I've come to despise you. You didn't want an honest prince. You couldn't appreciate the rose or the nightingale. But you could kiss the swineherd for a musical toy. Now you have what you deserve!"

With that he went into his kingdom, shut the door, and bolted it. Now indeed she could stand outside and sing –

> *"Ach, du lieber Augustin,*
> *All is gone, gone, gone!"*

THE PIXIE AT THE GROCER'S

THERE ONCE WAS A REAL STUDENT. He lived in the attic and owned nothing. There once was a real grocer. He lived on the ground floor and owned the whole house. A pixie chose to stay with him, because each Christmas Eve he was given a bowl of porridge with a large lump of butter in the middle! That was what the grocer had to offer, so the pixie stayed in the shop and it was most instructive.

One evening, the student came in by the back door to buy himself some cheese and a candle. He had no one to send to fetch it so he came himself. They gave him what he asked for, he paid for it, and received a "good evening" nod from the grocer and his wife. She was a woman who could do more than nod, she was a regular chatterbox! The student nodded back and then he stood quite still reading the scrap of paper wrapped around the cheese. It was a page, torn out of an old book which ought not to have been torn at all, an old book full of poetry.

"There are more!" said the grocer, "I gave an old woman some coffee beans for the book. For sixpence you can have the rest of it."

"Thanks," said the student, "Let me have it instead of the cheese! I can eat my bread without it. It would be a shame to tear the whole book to pieces. You are a spendid man, a practical man, but you have no more sense of poetry than that barrel!"

This was a rude thing to say, particularly to the barrel, but the grocer laughed and the student laughed, for it was only said in fun. The pixie was annoyed that anyone should talk like that to a grocer who was a landlord and sold the finest butter.

That night, when the grocery was locked, and everybody in bed except the student, the pixie sneaked in and stole the wife's chatterbox. She did not need it while she slept, and whatever object he gave it to in the house was given the power of speech, and was able to express its thoughts and feelings just as well as the wife herself. But only one person at a time could have it and that was a blessing, for otherwise they would all be talking at once.

The pixie put the chatterbox on the barrel, in which all the old newspapers were kept. "Is it really true," he asked, "that you have no idea of poetry?"

"Of course I do," said the barrel. "Poetry is that stuff on the bottom of the last page of the newspaper and is cut out! I should imagine that there's more poetry in me than in the student, and I'm only a humble barrel compared with the grocer!"

The pixie put the chatterbox on the coffee grinder next. My goodness, how it ran on! Then he put it on the butter churn and on the till. Everybody agreed with the barrel, and what the majority agrees upon must be respected.

"Now I'm going to give the student a piece of my mind!" And silently the pixie stole up the kitchen stairs to the attic where the student lived. There was a light on in there, and the pixie peeped through the keyhole and saw the student reading the tattered book from downstairs. But how light it was in there! Out of the book rose a bright beam which became a trunk, and then became a mighty tree, which rose high in the air spreading its branches wide above the student. The leaves were all so fresh and each blossom was the head of a lovely girl, some with dark gleaming eyes, others with eyes of a clear and wondrous blue. Each fruit was a shining star, and the most delightful singing could be heard.

The little pixie had never imagined, much less seen or felt, such splendour before. So he remained standing there on tiptoe, staring and staring until the light inside went out. No doubt the student had blown out the lamp before going to bed, but the little pixie remained because the song could still be heard, so soft and lovely, a beautiful lullaby for the student as he lay down to sleep.

"It's wonderful up here!" said the little pixie. "I never expected it. I think I will stay with the student!" And then he thought it over – and thought it over sensibly, and sighed, "But the student has no porridge!" And he left – yes, he went downstairs again to the grocer's. And it was a good thing he did, because the barrel had nearly worn out the wife's chatterbox, by listing from first to last everything it had inside. It was just about to roll over and repeat it all from the other end when the pixie arrived and took the chatterbox back to the grocer's wife. But from then on the whole shop, from the till to the firewood agreed with the barrel, respected it and had such faith in it that when, in the evening, the grocer read out from the art and theatre reviews in his newspaper, they all thought these were the barrel's own opinions.

But the little pixie no longer sat quietly listening to all the wisdom and reasoning downstairs. No, as soon as the light shone in the attic, the beams dragged him upstairs like strong anchor ropes. He had to run up and look in through the keyhole. And there he stood surrounded by a sense of grandeur, such as we feel when standing by the rolling ocean, when in a storm God walks over it. The pixie burst into tears. He could not explain why he wept, but the tears brought him such a blessed peace! How wonderful it would be to sit with the student under that tree, but that could never be – he was content with the keyhole. He was still standing on the landing when the autumn wind blew in through the little skylight and it was so cold, so cold. But the little fellow only noticed it when the light went out in the attic and the music was swept away on the wind. Ooh! Then he felt cold and hurried downstairs to his snug warm nook, where he was so comfortable. And when the Christmas porridge arrived with a big lump of butter – well, then the grocer was lord and master!

One night the pixie was woken by a dreadful noise coming from the street. People were banging on the shutters, the watchman's whistle was blowing; there was a big fire, the entire street was alight. Was this house on fire or was it the neighbour's? Where? It was terrifying! The grocer's wife panicked and took her gold earrings off and put them in her pocket so that at least something was saved. The grocer ran to find his stocks and shares and the maid ran to get her silk shawl, the one she had saved her wages for. Everyone wanted to save their most precious possession. So did the little pixie. In two bounds he was upstairs in the attic.

The student was standing calmly by the open window looking out at the fire. It was in the house opposite. The little pixie swept the precious book off the table, put it inside his red knitted hat and held on to it with both hands. The most valuable treasure in the house was saved! Then he dashed off, out onto the roof, and all the way up the chimney, and there he sat lit by the burning house across the street, both hands clutching his red hat that held the treasure. Now he knew where his heart lay, to whom he really belonged. But when at last the fire was out, and he again had his wits about him – well, "I shall divide myself between them!" he said. "I cannot abandon the grocer altogether, because of the porridge!"

And that is entirely human! We, too, go to the grocer – because of the porridge.

THE LITTLE MATCH GIRL

It was terribly cold. Snow was falling and it was beginning to get dark. It was also the last evening of the year, New Year's Eve. In this cold and in this darkness, a little girl walked in the street. A poor little girl, bareheaded and barefoot. Well, she had been wearing slippers when she left home, but what good was that? They were very big slippers; they used to belong to her mother and, they were so big that the little girl had lost them when she hurried across the street between two carriages that were rushing by. One slipper could not be found and a boy ran away with the other, saying he wanted it for a cradle when he had children himself.

There she walked, this little girl, on her small bare feet that were red and blue with cold. In an old apron she was carrying bundles of matches and she had one bunch of them in her hand. Nobody had bought any from her all day long. Nobody had given her a single coin. She was frozen and hungry and looked so discouraged, the poor little thing! The snowflakes fell on her long fair hair which curled beautifully around her neck, but she was certainly not thinking of the way she looked. Lights were shining from all the windows and there was a lovely smell of roast goose in the street. It was New Year's Eve, after all – and that was what she was thinking about.

In a corner between two houses, where one protruded a bit more than the other, she huddled down on the ground. She tucked her little legs beneath her but felt even colder, and she dared not go home as she had not sold any matches and no one had given her a penny. Her father would beat her, and besides it was cold at home; they had only a bare roof over them and even though they had stuffed the biggest holes with straw and rags, the wind still whistled right in. Her small hands were almost dead with cold. Oh, a match would be a comfort. If only she dared to pull one from the bunch and strike it on the wall to warm her fingers. She pulled one out. *Ritsch!* How it sparkled, how it burned! It was a clear warm flame, just like a little candle when she held her hand around it. But a curious candle! It seemed to the little girl that she sat in front of a large iron stove with brass facings and shiny brass knobs. The fire burned so deliciously and how it warmed! But what was that happening! The little girl had just stretched out her feet to warm them as well when the flame went out and the stove disappeared. There she sat with the little stub of the burnt-out match in her hand.

She struck a new one. It burned, it blazed, and where the light lit up the wall, it made it as transparent as gauze; she looked straight into a room where a table was set with a shining white tablecloth and with fine dishes; a roast goose, stuffed with prunes and apples steamed deliciously! And what was even more miraculous, the goose jumped from the dish and waddled across the floor, with the knife and fork in its back, right up to the poor child. At that very moment the match went out and there was nothing to be seen but the thick cold wall.

She lit another. Now she sat under the loveliest Christmas tree, even bigger and more richly decorated than the one she had seen through the glass door at the wealthy grocer's house last Christmas. A thousand candles burned on the green branches, and coloured pictures, like those in shop windows, looked down on her. The little child stretched up both hands – the match went out but as she watched, the Christmas candles rose high, high up in the air. She saw that they had become brilliant stars. One of them fell, making a long fiery trail across the sky.

"Now someone is dying," said the little girl, for her old dead grandmother, the only one who had ever been kind to her, had told her that when a star falls, a soul goes up to God.

Again she struck a match against the wall. It cast a pool of light all around and at the centre of the glow stood her old grandmother, so clear and luminous, so gentle and lovely.

"Granny!" cried the little child. "Oh, take me with you! I know you will be gone when the match burns out; gone like the warm stove, the lovely goose and the wonderful big Christmas tree!" Quickly she struck all the matches left in the bunch for she wanted to hold on to her Granny. The matches burned with such brilliance; it became brighter than daylight. Granny had never before looked so large, so beautiful. She lifted the little girl up in her arms and they flew high, high up, in radiance and happiness; up to where there was no cold, no hunger and no fear. They were with God!

But in the cold morning, there in the corner by the house sat the little girl, with rosy cheeks, and a smile on her lips – dead, frozen to death on the last night of the old year. New Year's Day dawned on the little corpse, sitting there with her matches, one bunch of them nearly all burnt up. She was trying to keep warm, people said. Nobody knew what beauty she had seen, in what glory she had gone with her old grandmother, into the joy of the New Year!

THE EMPEROR'S NEW CLOTHES

MANY YEARS AGO there lived an emperor who was so immensely fond of beautiful new clothes that he spent all his money on being splendidly dressed. He had no interest in his soldiers; he did not care for the theatre or for drives in the park except, and only, for showing off his new clothes. He had a robe for every hour of the day, and just as it might be said of some king, "He is in his council," it was always said here, "The Emperor is in his wardrobe!"

Much festivity went on in the big city where he lived, and many strangers arrived there every day. One such day there came two swindlers; they claimed to be weavers and said that they knew how to weave the most wonderful cloth imaginable. Not only were the colours and patterns something uncommonly beautiful to see, but also clothes sewn from their cloth had the extraordinary quality of being invisible to anyone either badly suited for his position or unforgivably stupid.

"Well those, of course, would be marvellous clothes," thought the Emperor. "Wearing those, I could discover who in my empire is not fit for the post he holds; I could tell the wise from the stupid. Yes, that cloth must be woven for me at once!" And he paid the two swindlers a lot of money in order that they could begin their work.

They actually did set up two looms, then pretended to be working, though they had absolutely nothing in the frames. Straight away, they demanded the finest silk and the most magnificent gold thread; this they put into their own bags, though still working their empty looms even far into the night.

"Now I should certainly like to know how far along they are with that cloth!" thought the Emperor. But it made him a bit uneasy to think that anyone stupid or at all unsuited for his position would be unable to see it – not that he himself need worry (he felt pretty confident about that!). All the same he had better send someone else first to see how matters stood. The whole city knew of the extraordinary powers invested in this cloth, and everyone was eager to see how inefficient or stupid his neighbour was.

"I will send my trustworthy old Prime Minister to the weavers," said the Emperor to himself. "He, better than anyone, will be able to see how the cloth looks, for he has good sense and nobody fills his post better than he!"

So off he went, the trusted old Prime Minister, to the hall where the two swindlers sat and worked at their empty looms. "Good heavens!" thought the old man, opening his eyes very wide. "I can't see a thing!" but he didn't say that.

Both swindlers begged him to be good enough to step up close, then asked, was it not a beautiful pattern and were not the colours delightful? All the time they were pointing at the empty loom and the poor old minister kept peering as hard as he could, but he could see nothing, for there was nothing. "Good gracious me!" he thought. "Could I possibly be stupid? I never thought I was. Nobody must ever know! Or is it possible that I am badly suited to my office? Oh, no, it will never do for me to admit that I do not see the material!"

"Well, you say nothing about it," said the one who was weaving.

"Oh, why it's charming! Absolutely adorable!" said the old minister, squinting through his spectacles. "This pattern! And these colours! Yes, I shall certainly report to the Emperor that it pleases me enormously!"

"Ah, we are happy to hear that!" said both weavers, and then they commented on the curious design and the colours, naming them. The old minister listened carefully so that he might be able to repeat it all when he got home to the Emperor – and that's just what he did.

Now the swindlers demanded more money, more silk and gold, which they needed for the weaving. They put everything into their own pockets; not a single thread went on the loom. But they continued as before, weaving on the empty loom.

Soon the Emperor sent yet another honest official to see how the weaving was getting along and whether the cloth might be ready soon. He fared no better than the Prime Minister. He looked and looked, but as there was nothing but the empty frames, he could see nothing.

"There now! Isn't that a piece of handsome stuff!" said both swindlers, pointing out and explaining the lovely design, which did not exist at all.

"Stupid I am not!" thought the man. "Am I then unfit for my excellent position? That's curious! Of course it won't do to let anyone suspect!" Whereupon he praised the cloth he did not see and assured them of his delight in the pretty shades and lovely patterns. "Yes, it's absolutely adorable!" he told the Emperor.

The whole city was talking about the marvellous cloth.

The Emperor now wanted to see it for himself while it was still on the loom. With a whole crowd of selected gentlemen, among which were the two poor old officials who had been there before, he visited the crafty swindlers who were weaving away for all they were worth, but without shred or thread.

"Yes, is it not *magnifique?*" asked the two honest officials. "May it please Your Majesty, observe . . . Such a design! Such colours!" And they pointed to the empty loom, believing that others could probably see the cloth.

"What's this!" thought the Emperor. "I see nothing! But that's awful! Am I stupid? Am I not fit to be Emperor? That would be the most appalling thing that could ever befall me! – Oh, it's very beautiful!" said the Emperor. "It has our most gracious approval!" And he nodded contentedly, looking at the empty loom; he was not going to admit that he could not see anything. His whole retinue, all the people he had brought along, looked and looked but had no more success than anybody else. However, like the Emperor, they said, "Oh, it's very beautiful!" And they advised him to use this fabulous new material for a suit he could wear for the first time in the grand procession that would soon take place. "It's *magnifique!* Delicious! *Superbe!*" were the comments running from mouth to mouth, and everyone was just enchanted with the whole thing. The Emperor awarded each of the swindlers a Knight's Cross to hang from his buttonhole, and bestowed on them the title of Knights-of-the-Loom.

The entire night before the morning of the procession the two swindlers sat up with more than sixteen candles burning. People could see that they were busy trying to get the Emperor's new

clothes finished in time. They pretended to be taking the cloth from the loom; they snipped at the air with large scissors; they sewed away with needles without thread; and at last they said, "There! The clothes are ready!"

The Emperor, with his most distinguished gentlemen-in-waiting, arrived in person. The two Knights-of-the-Loom each lifted an arm, as if they were holding something between them, and said, "Look, here are the trousers! Here's the frock coat! Here's the robe!" and so forth and so on. "It's as light as a cobweb! It feels as if one had nothing on at all; but that's just the beauty of it!"

"Quite!" answered all the gentlemen.

But they could see nothing, for there was nothing.

67

"Would it please Your Gracious Majesty to remove your clothes now?" asked the swindlers. "Then we shall fit the new ones on Your Majesty over here by the large mirror!"

The Emperor took off all his clothes, and the rascals pretended to be handing him each piece of the new ones they were supposed to have sewn. They reached around his middle and made motions as if tying something on; that was the train, and the Emperor twisted and turned in front of the mirror.

"Good gracious me, how it suits Your Majesty! How nicely it fits!" they all said. "What a pattern! Such colours! These are elegant clothes!"

"The canopy to be carried above Your Majesty in the procession is waiting outside," said the Imperial-Chief-Master-of-Ceremonies.

"Yes, as you see, I'm all ready!" said the Emperor. "Doesn't it fit well?"

And he made yet another turn in front of the mirror, for he wanted it to look as if he were really admiring his finery.

The chamberlains who were supposed to carry the train ran their hands along the floor as if to lift the train; then walked off holding the air, not daring to let anyone suspect that they could not see anything.

And so the Emperor walked in the procession under the lovely canopy, while all the crowds in the street and all the people at their windows said, "Heavens! How marvellous the Emperor's new clothes look! Such a beautiful train on those robes! How exquisitely it fits!" No one wanted it thought that he could not see anything, as that would make him somebody who was either very stupid or badly fitted for his position.

Never before had the Emperor's clothes been such a success.

"But he has nothing on!" said a little child.

"Good heavens, listen to the voice of innocence!" said the father, and the child's remark was whispered from one to another.

"He has nothing on! That's what a little child is saying. 'He has nothing on!'"

"He has nothing on!" shouted everybody in the end. And the Emperor cringed inside himself, for it seemed to him that they were right; but he thought like this: "I shall have to go through with the procession."

And then he held himself even more proudly erect, and the chamberlains walked on behind him carrying the train that was not there at all.

THE SWEETHEARTS

THE TOP AND THE BALL lay in the drawer together with some other toys, and the top said to the ball, "Why don't we become sweethearts? After all we are lying in the same drawer!" But the ball, which was made of morocco leather, and just as conceited as any fine young lady, would not even answer him.

The little boy who owned the toys came the next day and painted the top red and yellow. He hammered a brass nail into its middle, and now the top looked just splendid as it spun around.

"Look at me!" he said to the ball. "What do you say now? Shouldn't we become sweethearts? We suit each other so well. You jump and I dance! Nobody could be happier than we two would be!"

"Indeed, is that what you believe?" said the ball. "I don't think you are aware that my father and mother were morocco leather slippers, or that I have cork inside!"

"Yes, but I am made of mahogany!" said the top. "The mayor himself turned me on his own lathe, and he took great pleasure in it!"

"Am I expected to believe that?" said the ball.

"May I never be whipped if I lie!" answered the top.

"You speak well for yourself!" said the ball, "and yet I must refuse. I am practically half-engaged to a swallow! Every time I go up in the air, it sticks its head out of the nest, and says 'Will you? Will you?' My inner self has accepted, and that is as good as half an engagement. But I promise I shall never forget you!"

"Yes, that will be a great help!" said the top. And they stopped talking.

The next day the ball was taken outside; the top watched her soar high up in the air just like a bird, until she was out of sight. She kept coming down, but bounced back up again each time she touched the

ground. This may have been due to longing for the swallow or maybe it was because she had a cork inside. The ninth time the ball disappeared and never came back again. The boy searched and searched but she was gone.

"I am sure I know where she is," sighed the top. "She is in the swallow's nest and is married to the swallow!"

The more the top thought about it, the more he loved the ball: just because he could not have her, the more he loved her. The fact that she had chosen another made it even worse, and as he danced about and spun around, he was always thinking about her, and in his thoughts she became lovelier and lovelier. In this way many years passed – and so it became no more than an old love affair.

The top was no longer young. But, one day, it was painted gold all over. It had never looked more splendid. It was now a gold top and spun so, that it whirred. This was really something! But suddenly it spun too far and – it was gone!

They searched and searched, even down in the cellar, but it was not to be found.

Where could it be?

It had spun into the dustbin, where all manner of things lay; cabbage stalks, gravel and sweepings, that had come from the gutter on the roof.

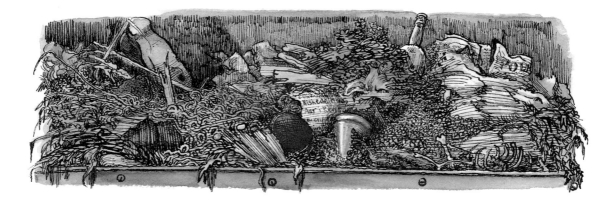

"This is a fine place to lie! I shall soon lose my gold paint here. And what sort of riff-raff have I landed amongst!" He scowled at a long cabbage stalk, much too closely peeled, and at an odd round object which looked like an old apple. But it was not an apple, it was an old ball which had spent many years up in the gutter and where the water had soaked through it.

"Thank God, at last someone of one's own kind to talk to!" said the ball, contemplating the gold top. "Actually, I am made of morocco leather, stitched by the hands of gentlewomen, and with a cork inside, but you would not think so seeing me now! I was about to marry a swallow, but I fell into the gutter and have lain there soaking for five years. Believe me, for a lady, that is a long time!"

But the top did not say anything. He thought of his old love, and the more he heard, the more he realised that it was she.

Suddenly the maid came to empty the dustbin; "Hey-ho, there is the gold top!" she said.

And so the top was back in the parlour again, the object of much respect and esteem. But nothing more was ever heard of the ball, and the top never mentioned his past love again.

Love fades, especially when the loved one has been soaking for five years in a gutter; you can't be expected to recognise her if you meet her in the dustbin.

The Fir Tree

OUT IN THE WOODS stood a fir tree, such a pretty fir tree. It was well placed; the sun could reach it. There was plenty of air, and around it grew many larger comrades, both fir and pine. But the little fir tree was so impatient to grow, it gave no thought to the warm sun and the fresh air. It took no notice of the farm children who walked about chatting when they came to pick strawberries or raspberries. They often arrived with a pot full and strung strawberries on a straw. They would sit down by the little tree and say, "Oh, look how pretty that little one is!" This the tree tried not to hear.

One year later it had grown a set of long new branches, and the next year yet another, for with a fir tree you can always tell how many years it has been growing by the number of sets it has.

"Oh, if only I could be a big tree like the others," sighed the little tree. "Then I could spread out my branches and with my top see out in the wide world. The birds would build nests in my branches and when the wind blew I would nod in a dignified fashion like the others over there."

It took no pleasure from the sun, or the birds, or the rosy clouds sailing above it in the mornings and evenings.

In winter, when the snow lay white and sparkling all around, a hare often came and jumped right over it, and that was very annoying! But two winters passed, and by the third the tree was so big that the hare had to walk around it. Oh, to grow, to grow and become big and old, that must be the most wonderful thing in the world, thought the tree.

In the autumn, woodsmen came to fell some of the biggest trees. This happened every year, and the young fir tree which was now quite grown up shuddered as the magnificent great trees fell creaking and crashing to the ground. Their branches were lopped off and they looked quite naked, long and thin, almost unrecognisable. They were then loaded onto carts, and horses dragged them away, out of the forest.

Where were they taken? What would happen to them? In the spring, when the swallows and the stork came, the tree asked them, "Do you know where they were taken? Have you seen them?"

The swallows knew nothing but the stork looked thoughtful, nodded his head and said, "Yes, I think so! I met many new ships when I flew from Egypt. These ships had splendid masts. I dare say it was them, they smelled of fir. They sent their greetings. They looked stately, very stately!"

"Oh, if only I were big enough to fly away over the sea! What is it like, this sea? What does it look like?"

"Well, that might become a long-winded explanation," said the stork, and he walked away.

"Enjoy your youth!" said the sunbeams. "Rejoice in your fresh growth and the young life which is in you!" And the wind kissed the tree and the dew wept tears over it, but the fir tree understood none of this.

At Christmas-time, quite young trees were felled, trees not even as big or as old as this fir tree which knew no peace but was always longing to be away. These young trees, always the most beautiful,

kept their branches. They were loaded on carts, and horses pulled them away, out of the forest.

"Where are they going?" asked the fir tree. "They are no bigger than I, one was even much smaller. Why did they keep all their branches? Where are they going?"

"We know! We know!" chirped the sparrows. "We've looked through the windows in town! We know where they are going! Oh, they are being taken to the greatest glory and splendour imaginable. We have looked through the windows and seen them planted in the middle of warm sitting rooms, all decorated with the loveliest things; golden apples, honey-cakes, toys and hundreds and hundreds of candles!"

"And then?" asked the fir tree, quivering in every branch. "And then? What happens next?"

"Well, that's all we saw! It was wonderful!"

"I wonder if I was born for such a glorious road!" rejoiced the tree. "It's even better than sailing across the sea. I ache with longing!

If only it were Christmas. I have grown tall and full, like those taken away last year! Oh, if only I were already on the cart! If only I were in that warm room in all that glory and splendour! And then? Well, something even better, even more wonderful would happen. Why else would they decorate me like that? There's bound to be something even greater, even more wonderful in store! But what? Oh, how I ache! How I yearn! I don't know what's the matter with me."

"Rejoice in me!" said the air and the sunlight. "Rejoice in your fresh youth out in the free open air!"

But the tree did nothing of the kind. It grew and grew. Winter and summer it stood there; green, dark green. People who saw it said, "That's a lovely tree!" and at Christmas-time it was felled before all the others. The axe cut deep, through the heart, and the tree fell to the ground with a sigh; it felt such pain and weakness. It could not think of happiness; it was sad to be leaving home, from

the spot where it had sprouted. It knew that it would never again see the dear old friends, the little bushes and flowers around it, yes — perhaps not even the birds. The departure was not pleasant at all.

The tree only came to itself when it had been unloaded in a courtyard along with the other trees, and heard a man say, "Yes, that one is splendid! We don't want any other!"

Then two footmen in full livery arrived and carried the fir tree into a beautiful large hall. Portraits hung on the walls, and by the big tiled stove stood large Chinese vases with lions on the lids; there were rocking chairs, silken sofas, great tables laden with picture books and toys worth a hundred times a hundred crowns; at least that's what the children said. The fir tree was planted in a big tub filled with sand, but no one could see it was a tub for a green cloth was draped around it, and it was placed on a large colourful carpet. Oh, how the tree trembled! What was going to happen now? Servants and young ladies were busy decorating it. On one branch they hung little nets cut out of coloured paper, every net filled with sweets; golden apples and walnuts hung as if they were growing there; and over a hundred small candles, red, blue and white, were fastened to the branches. Dolls that looked perfectly life-like – such as the tree had never seen before – floated in the greenery, and all the way up on the very top was placed a big star of gold tinsel. It was magnificent, absolutely magnificent.

"Tonight," they all said, "tonight it will be dazzling!"

"Oh," thought the tree. "If only it were evening! If only the candles were lit! And then, what will happen then? I wonder if the trees from the forest will come to see me? Will the sparrows fly to the window? Am I to strike roots here and stand decorated, winter and summer?"

Yes, it had already learned a lot, but it had a bad case of barkache from sheer longing, and barkache is just as bad for a tree as a headache is for us.

Now the candles were lit. What brilliance! What splendour! All the tree's branches quivered so that one of the candles set fire to the greenery. It hurt badly.

"Heaven help us!" screamed the young ladies and quickly put out the fire. Now the tree dared not even tremble. Oh, it was dreadful! It was so afraid of losing any of its finery, it was quite dizzy in all that

glory – and now both folding doors opened and a flock of children burst into the room as if they would overturn the tree. Their elders followed behind, somewhat more composed. The little ones stood still as mice. But only for a moment: then they were shouting with joy again so that the room rang with the noise. They danced around the tree and picked off the presents; one after the other, the presents were plucked off.

"What is it they are doing? What is going to happen?" thought the tree.

The candles burned right down to the branches, and as they burned down they were put out. Then the children were allowed to plunder the tree.

Oh, they rushed in on the tree so that all its branches groaned. Had it not been attached to the ceiling by the top with the gold star it would have fallen down.

The children danced around with their splendid toys. Nobody looked at the tree, except the old nurse who went peering in between the branches, but that was just to see if perhaps one more fig or apple was left.

"A story! A story!" shouted the children and pulled a little fat man towards the tree. He sat down directly under it. "That way we're in greenery," he said, "and the tree might do worse than listen in! But I'm going to tell only one story. Do you want to hear the one about Wivvy-Divvy or the one about Humpty-Dumpty who fell down the stairs and still gained the throne and won the princess?"

"Wivvy-Divvy!" screamed some. "Humpty-Dumpty!" screamed others. There was such constant screaming and shouting; only the fir tree remained silent and thought, "Am I not to join in at all? Not to do anything at all?" But it had joined in; it had done what it had to do.

The man told of Humpty Dumpty who fell down the stairs and still gained the throne and won the princess. The children clapped their hands and shouted, "Tell us more! Tell us more!" But they only got the one about "Humpty-Dumpty". The fir tree stood quite still and thoughtful; none of the birds out in the forest had ever told of such things. "Humpty-Dumpty fell down the stairs and still won the princess! Yes, well, that's the way of the world!" thought the fir tree, believing it all to be true because such a fine man had told the story. "Ah yes, who knows! Perhaps I too shall fall down the stairs and win a princess!" And it looked forward to the next day when it was to be hung with lights and toys, gold and fruits.

In the morning, a servant and a boy came in.

"Now the party will begin all over again," thought the tree. But they dragged it out of the hall, up the stairs and into the attic, and left it in a dark corner where no daylight entered. "What can this mean?" thought the tree. "What am I to do here? What stories will they tell me here?" and it leaned against the wall and thought and

thought. It had plenty of time; days and nights passed. Nobody went up there, and when finally somebody did come, it was to put some large crates in the corner. The tree stood well hidden and, most probably, quite forgotten

"It will be winter out there now!" thought the tree. "The ground will be hard and covered with snow. People cannot plant me and that's why I must stay up here, protected until spring. How thoughtful! Aren't people good! If only it were not so dark and so terribly lonesome – not even a little hare. It was really so pretty out there in the forest when the snow lay over everything, and the hare jumped by. Yes, even when it jumped over me, though I didn't like that then. This is a terribly lonesome place up here."

"Squeak, squeak," said a little mouse suddenly and scurried out, followed by another little one. They sniffed the fir tree and slipped in amongst its branches.

"It's awfully cold," said the small mice. "Otherwise it's a blessing to be here, don't you agree, you old fir tree?"

"I'm not old!" said the fir tree. "Many are much older than I!"

81

"Where do you come from?" asked the mice. "And what do you know?" They were terribly curious. "Tell us about the loveliest place in the world. Have you been there? Have you been in the larder, where there are cheeses on the shelves and hams hanging from the ceiling, where one can dance on wax candles and go in lean and come out fat?"

"I don't know that place," said the tree. "But I know the woods, where the sun shines and where the birds sing!" And it told them all about its youth. The little mice had never heard about such things. They listened very carefully and said, "Goodness, what a lot you have seen! How happy you have been!"

"Me!" said the fir tree, and pondered on its own story. "Yes, in a way those were quite good times." But then it told of Christmas Eve, when it was decorated with cakes and candles.

"Oh!" said the small mice. "How happy you have been, you old fir tree!"

"I'm not at all old!" said the tree. "I only arrived from the forest this winter. I'm in my very prime. It's just that my growth has been stunted."

"You tell your stories so wonderfully," said the small mice, and the next night they came with four other little mice to hear the tree tell stories. And the more it told, the more it remembered everything and thought, "Those were really quite enjoyable times. But they will come back, they will come back! Humpty-Dumpty fell down the stairs and still won the princess. Maybe I too can win a princess," and the fir tree thought of a lovely little birch tree which grew in the woods. To the fir tree that was a truly lovely princess.

"Who's Humpty-Dumpty?" asked the little mice. And the fir tree told them the whole fairy tale. It remembered every word, and the little mice were ready to jump to the top of the tree in their excitement. The next night many more mice came, and on the Sunday even two rats, but they said that the story was not amusing, and that saddened the small mice because now they also enjoyed it less.

"Do you only know that one story?" asked the rats.

"Only that one," answered the tree. "I heard it on the happiest night of my life, but at the time I didn't realise how happy I was."

"It is an extremely poor story! Don't you know any about bacon and wax candles? No pantry stories?"

"No," said the tree.

"Well, thank you for nothing!" replied the rats and went home.

At last even the little mice stopped coming and that made the tree sigh, "It really was very pleasant having those tiny nimble mice sitting round me, listening to what I told them. Now that, too, is over! But I shall remember to enjoy myself when I'm taken out again."

But when would that be? Well, it happened one morning. People came to bustle about in the attic. The crates were moved, the tree was dragged out – they did throw it down a bit hard – but at once a boy pulled it out to the stairs where there was daylight.

"Life begins anew!" thought the tree. It felt the fresh air, the first rays of sunshine, and suddenly it was out in the courtyard. Everything happened so quickly the tree quite forgot to look at itself, there was so much to see all around. The courtyard bordered on a garden and everything in there was in bloom. The roses hung fresh and fragrant over the little fence. The linden trees were in flower and the swallows flew about saying "Tweet-tweet, my husband has come home!" But they were not talking about the fir tree.

"Now I can live again!" it rejoiced, spreading its branches wide. Alas! They were all withered and yellow and naked. It lay in a corner amongst nettles and weeds. The gold paper star, still sitting on the top, glittered in the clear sunshine.

A few merry children were playing in the courtyard, the same children who had danced around the tree at Christmas and rejoiced in it. One of the youngest ran over and tore off the gold star.

"Look what's still on that nasty old Christmas tree!" he said and stamped on the branches so that they crackled under his boots.

The tree looked at all the wealth of flowers in the fresh garden and it looked at itself, wishing that it had stayed in the dark corner of the attic. It thought of its fresh youth in the forest, of that joyful Christmas Eve and of the little mice who had listened so happily to the story of Humpty-Dumpty.

"It's over! It's over!" said the poor tree. "If only I could have enjoyed it while it lasted! It's over! It's over!"

Then the servant came and chopped the tree into little pieces. It made quite a heap, lying there, and it made a fine fire under the copper in the scullery; and it sighed so deeply, each sigh was like a little pistol shot. This made the playing children come running and they sat down in front of the fire, staring into it and shouting "Bang! Bang!" But at every pop, which was a deep sigh, the tree remembered a summer day in the woods, a winter night out under the brilliant stars. It thought of Christmas Eve and Humpty-Dumpty, the only fairy-tale it had heard and knew how to tell – and then the tree was all burnt up.

The boys were playing in the courtyard, and the smallest one had the gold star the tree had worn on its happiest night pinned to his chest. Now that was over, and it was all over with the tree, and so it is with the story. It's over, over. That's what happens to stories.

TWELVE BY COACH

IT WAS FREEZING so hard it creaked; clear starry weather with no wind. "Crash!" A flower pot was thrown against a street door. "Pzzzz-t!" They were shooting off fireworks to celebrate the New Year; it was New Year's Eve and the clock was striking.

"Tra-ta! Tra-ta!" That was the post horn. The big mail coach was stopping outside the city gate; it brought twelve passengers, that's all there was room for, every seat was taken.

"Hurrah! Hurrah!" sang the people in their houses where they were celebrating New Year's Eve. They stood up, raised their full glasses and drank a toast to the New Year.

"Health and happiness in the New Year!" they cried. "A little wife! Lots of money! No more nonsense!"

Yes, that is what people wished each other as they touched glasses and – the coach stopped at the gate with the visitors, the twelve travellers.

What sort of people were they? They came with passports and luggage, yes, presents for you and me and for all the people in town.

Who were these strangers? What did they want and what did they bring?

"Good morning!" they said to the sentry at the gate.

"Good morning!" he said. The clock had, after all, struck twelve.

"Your name? Your occupation?" the sentry asked of the first to step out of the coach.

"Look in my passport!" said the man. "I am I!" and he really was quite a character, dressed in a bearskin coat and wearing sleigh boots. "I am the hope of a great many people. Come tomorrow, I'm giving a New Year's party! I throw handfuls of shillings to people in the streets, I give presents, yes, and I give balls, thirty-one Grand Balls, I have only that many nights to dispose of. My ships are icebound, but my office is warm. I am a merchant and my name is January. I've brought nothing but bills with me."

Then came the next. He was a merrymaker, director of comedies, masquerades, and all kinds of entertainments imaginable.

"I intend to amuse others as well as myself, for I have the shortest life in the whole family. I shall only live to be twenty-eight. Well, perhaps I shall manage a leap into one day more; but who cares, hurrah!"

"You are not allowed to shout so loudly," said the sentry.

"Yes, I certainly am," said the man. "I am Prince Carnival and travel under the name Februarius."

Now came the third. He looked like fasting itself, but held his head high because he was related to the forty robbers and was a prophet of the weather; not a job to get fat on, which is why he was so keen on Lent. For decoration he had a bunch of violets in his buttonhole, but they were very small ones.

"Quick march, March!" shouted the fourth pushing the third. "Quick march into the guard house. They are serving punch! I can smell it!" But that was not true; he wanted to make an April-Fool of him, and that was the way the fourth began. He seemed a pert enough fellow with probably not much to do but celebrate holidays. "My moods are rather up and down," he said. "Rain and sunshine, moving in and moving out! I am an Estate Agent, I am an Undertaker, I can both laugh and weep. I have summer clothes in the suitcase, but it would be a mistake to put them on. Here I am! When I dress up, I wear silk stockings and carry a muff."

Now a lady stepped out of the coach.

"Miss May!" she announced. In summer clothes and galoshes, she wore a silk frock the colour of green beech leaves, anemones in her hair, and gave off such a fragrance of woodruff that the guard had to sneeze. "God bless you!" she said; that was her greeting. She was lovely! And she was a singer; not on the stage but in the fresh green woods. She sang there for her own pleasure. She carried small volumes of poetry in her sewing basket.

"Here comes the Mistress, the young Mistress!" they now shouted inside the coach, and out stepped a young lady, delicate, proud and beautiful. She was obviously well-born. She gave a party on the longest day of the year, to give people time to taste all the courses

served. She could afford a carriage of her own, yet she came in the mail coach like the others, to prove that she was not a snob. But she did not travel alone, she was accompanied by her younger brother, Julius.

He was a distinguished man, in summer clothes and wearing a panama hat. He brought light luggage only, anything else is a nuisance when it gets hot. He had packed merely a bathing cap and a pair of swimming trunks.

Now came Madame August. She dealt in fruit by the barrel, and owned many fish ponds: a lady-farmer in a grand crinoline. She was fat and hot, involved herself in everything, and brought beer kegs out to the field hands. "By the sweat of thy brow, shalt thou eat thy bread," she said.  "It says so in the Bible. Afterwards, by all means have your ball and your harvest festival!" She was a real mother.

Another man appeared, a painter by profession, a master colourist. The forests displayed his art: the leaves changed colour, beautifully, at his pleasure; his palette was red, yellow, brown. The master whistled like the black starling, was a hard worker and hung brownish-green hop plants around his beer mug for decoration – he had a keen eye for decoration. So here he was with his paints; that was all the luggage he had brought.

Now followed the gentleman-farmer who thought his month a time for sowing and ploughing and treating the soil, yes, and also for some of the pleasures of hunting and shooting. He had a retriever and a gun, and nuts in his game bag; rattle-click! What a lot of gear to bring along, and an English plough besides; he spoke of farm economics, but not much could be heard for all the coughing and snuffling from November who followed.

He had a head cold, a really bad cold, so bad that he used a sheet instead of a handkerchief! But he said that as soon as he'd cut some fire wood he would feel better. He was Master of the Guild of Woodcutters. His evenings were spent whittling skates; he knew that in a few weeks this amusing foot gear would come in handy.

Now came the last passenger, the little old woman with her coal brazier; she was cold, but her eyes sparkled like two bright stars. She was carrying a flower pot with a small fir tree in it. "I shall nurse it and care for it, so that it will grow tall by Christmas Eve, all the way from the floor to the ceiling, and sprout lighted candles, golden apples and paper decorations. The brazier will give out warmth like a stove, and I shall take the fairytale book out of my pocket and read aloud, so that all the children in the room are quiet.

"But the dolls on the tree will come alive and the little wax angel on the top of the tree will shake its gold paper wings and fly down from the green tip of the tree to kiss old and young in the room. Yes, even the poor children who stand outside singing the Christmas song about the star over Bethlehem."

"The coach may now drive on!" said the sentry. "We have all twelve. Let the next coach drive up."

"First send all twelve in to me!" said the captain on duty. "One at a time! I shall keep your passports. Each of you will be allowed one month. When that is over, I shall make a report on your behaviour in your passport, each one of you. Mr January, this way please."

And January walked in.

When a year has passed, I'll tell you what the twelve have brought us; you, me, all of us. I can't tell you yet, and the twelve probably can't either, for we live in strange times.